This edition published by Parragon Books Ltd in 2015 and distributed by

Parragon Inc.
440 Park Avenue South, 13th Floor
New York, NY 10016
www.parragon.com

ISBN 978-1-4723-9633-4

Printed in China

Disney
MINNIE

PaRragon

Bath · New York · Cologne · Melbourne · Delhi
Hong Kong · Shenzhen · Singapore · Amsterdam

One sunny day, Minnie Mouse was
walking her dog, Fifi, when she noticed
a sign posted on a fence.

"Look, Fifi, a dog show!" Minnie said
with excitement. "There are prizes, too.
Fifi, you should enter!"

DOG SHOW!
THIS SATURDAY
AT NOON IN THE PARK

PRIZES!

Minnie and Fifi went straight home to practice. After all, the show was only two days away!

As they practiced, Minnie grew more and more confident. Fifi was one very talented pup!

"Fifi, sit up!" said Minnie.
Fifi sat up proudly.
"Now, shake my hand."
Fifi held up a dainty paw.

"Good girl, Fifi!" said Minnie, shaking Fifi's paw. "Now, roll over."

Fifi sat up and let out a loud bark, "Ruff!"

"No, no," said Minnie. "You're supposed to bark when I say 'speak.'"

Fifi rolled over excitedly.

"Oh dear!" said Minnie. "We've got some work to do, Fifi!"

On the morning of the dog show, Minnie gave
Fifi a bath and dressed her in a red polka-dot bow.
"Now we match!" said Minnie happily. She and
Fifi walked down the street toward the town square.

All of a sudden, Fifi pulled at the leash
and began to race down the street.
"Ruff! Ruff!" Fifi barked. She was running
after a squirrel!

Minnie held on tight as Fifi chased the squirrel.
"Fifi, stop!" she cried.

But Fifi was too fast. Minnie watched in surprise
as Fifi slipped right out of her collar and disappeared
around the corner!

"Fifi!" Minnie cried. "Please come back!"

Minnie raced after Fifi. She turned the corner,
but Fifi was nowhere in sight.

Minnie searched and searched, but all she found
was the tiny, frightened squirrel.

"Oh, Fifi, where are you?" Minnie wondered.

Minnie raced home, hoping to
find Fifi waiting for her.
But Fifi wasn't there either.
Minnie called her best
friend, Daisy, to tell her
Fifi was lost.

"I'll be right there!"
said Daisy. "And I'll
bring Mickey, too!"

When Daisy and Mickey arrived at Minnie's house,
Minnie was very upset.

"Don't worry, Minnie," said Mickey. "We'll help you find her!"

"That's right," Daisy agreed. "I know just what to do. Let's go!"

Daisy called the town animal shelter right away.
"I want to report a missing dog," she told them.
"Her name is Fifi. When she disappeared, she was
wearing a red polka-dot bow."

Mickey and Minnie decided to make some signs.
They gathered supplies and got straight to work.

"Let's post them all around town," suggested Mickey. "Someone is sure to find Fifi!"

"Great idea, Mickey!" said Minnie.

Mickey and Minnie made lots of big, bold signs.

Minnie and her helpful friends went all around the neighborhood, calling for Fifi and posting the signs.

"Great work, everyone!" said Mickey.

"Now let's go back to your house, Minnie,"
suggested Daisy. "Fifi may have found her way home."
"Thank you both for helping me," said Minnie.
"We love Fifi, too!" said Mickey.

But when they reached Minnie's house, there was still no sign of her little dog.

"Poor Fifi," Minnie said. "Where could she be?"

Just then, Daisy had an idea. "I know! I'll send a message to all my friends, asking if they've seen Fifi," she said. "With everyone's help, I'm sure we'll find her!"

"Great thinking, Daisy!" cheered Mickey.

"Oh, thank you," said Minnie. "You two are such good friends."

"We have lost a tan and cream dog with a red polka-dot bow," Daisy wrote to her friends. "Please keep an eye out for her!"

Within minutes, Daisy started getting messages back.

I'll go out and look!

Poor thing. I'll keep an eye out.

Sure thing, Daisy!

Hey, Daisy! Does she look like this?

Suddenly, a picture came up on Daisy's phone. It was of a cute, little dog with a red polka-dot bow—and a big blue ribbon! It was Fifi!

"It's Fifi! It's Fifi!" Minnie cried.

Daisy sent a message back: "Yes! That's Fifi! Where is she?"

When the answer came, Daisy read the reply. "She's at the dog show!" she exclaimed.

Minnie raced toward the park with Mickey and Daisy right behind her.

DOG SHOW HERE TODAY!

"Ruff! Ruff!" barked Fifi happily when she saw Minnie.

"Oh, Fifi, I was so worried about you!" said Minnie. "How did you get here? And how did you win a blue ribbon?"

One of the judges came over to explain.
"Your dog arrived just as we began judging,"
he said. "Every time someone said 'sit,' your dog sat.
Every time someone said 'shake,' your dog held up
one of her paws. She deserved first place!"

Minnie smiled. "You clever little dog," she said.
"You're lucky no one said 'roll over'!"
Fifi sat up and barked, "Ruff!"
Minnie giggled and hugged her prize-winning dog.
"Oh, Fifi, you'll always win first place with me!"

The End